4th Time Lucky

4th Time Lucky

Rex Alistair

4th Time Lucky

For those in search of faeries.

I try not to think about how I got here. When I do take a moment to reminisce, I don't picture gold brick, China tea sets or warm, crackling fires. I picture a cold room with a high ceiling and a low-hanging light. I can see the neighbour's Christmas decorations through my window and I am wearing three jumpers to keep warm. The smell of the beef stew I had for dinner lingers in the air.

When I think about how I got here, I am sitting in my bedroom, in my second year at uni, pretending to work on a particularly boring essay.

There's a creak followed by a small exclamation as Dan lets himself into my room and biffs his head on the light. It swings violently, sending shadows flying across the room, as I hurriedly type out a garbage sentence and swivel around to face him.

Rex Alistair

Dan is unreasonably tall, and he definitely isn't fooled by me pretending to work, but he's polite and pretends he doesn't notice. The swinging light throws shadows around the straight lines of his face and he speaks in a tone that begs me to *please please please* agree with whatever he's about to ask.

"Kyle, do you wanna go on holiday with me and Matt this summer?" Dan says, running a hand through his short brown hair. "You'd be doing me a huge favour."

Ah, I think, *wingman duty*. I ask if he's planning to go to the Cotswolds. Dan has a massive hard-on for the Cotswolds. He lived there for a year or two as a kid and constantly fantasises about going back.

"We were thinking Broadway," he says.

I know Matt, and Dan's a good friend, so I agree.

That's how I got here.

The first time, you will need it.

Supposedly, we were in the middle of a heatwave, but we arrived in Broadway on the one day it decided to rain. I arrived at the cottage Matt had booked, looking rather like a drowned rat. In theory, my hair is dirty blonde and shaggy, but by the time I got there it was poo-coloured and pasted flat to my head. Dan was already there, and he laughed and let me in.

"Should've got the shampoo out and had a shower," he said. I gave him a dirty look and stashed my bike in the laundry room. "You're in the small room, by the way."

I'd already agreed to take the small room, but thanked him for reminding me. The room wasn't so bad on its own. There was a small bed and a dresser with a lamp on top, which was all I needed from a bedroom, but everything was _white_. The walls, the floor, the bedsheets, the furniture. I was terrified to track dirt in by mistake. I think that's why I don't like these all-white modern aesthetics. Just thinking about how much cleaning I'd have to do gives me a stomach ache.

I immediately set about unpacking and stowed my suitcase under the bed. In that short time, Matt had evidently fallen asleep on the sofa. Dan and I looked at each other, and agreed to bully him later for renting a 'cottage' that was actually just a gold-brick house on the outskirts of the village. Poor Dan and his cottagecore summer romance fantasies. "Better luck next time," I told him. He'd need it if Matt was in charge of booking again.

We tried to watch something on the telly, but there was nothing on that we wanted to watch, so when the rain turned from a downpour to a drizzle, I said, "Want to go for a wander?"

"I mean, we have to do a grocery shop anyway," Dan said. Then he gave me an awkward look and added, "I forgot my toothbrush."

Well, one of us was bound to forget something. I wrote a note to tell Matt where we were going, and we headed off.

Here's the thing about Broadway: the main part of it is a long, wide road lined with shops. This is fine— it actually makes shopping rather simple—except that the grocery store is set back from the main road and hidden behind a chippy. We managed to walk past it twice before we noticed a sign pointing us in the right direction.

Did we feel stupid? Of course we felt stupid. Were we going to tell Matt? Absolutely not. He'd bully us off the planet for it.

After making a successful grocery run, we decided to stop in a tearoom to eat our shame away. We were somewhat spoiled for choice since there are so many tearooms in the Cotswolds. I'm sure they make up at least half the buildings in Broadway alone. We settled on the first one we came to.

Dan approached the counter, saying he'd buy us a round, while I chose a place to sit. I found a table near the window, next to a leaflet stand, and began to pick up as many leaflets as I could. I've always loved going through them, ever since I was a kid. I had a lovely big pile by the time Dan got back to the table.

"Give us that one," he said, pointing to a leaflet for Broadway Tower. I'd already looked through it, so I slid it over to him and returned to my hoard. There was a small booklet full of nature trails, walks, and so on, and I showed it to Dan.

"I want to do a cycling trail at some point," I told him.

Dan wasn't into cycling, but he said, "You should take Matt with you. He loves stuff like that. Bike's on its last legs though."

"Is it?"

"Yeah, can't do much anymore. Too tired."

I slapped him with a leaflet advertising an enchanted forest. *Two tired.* For God's sake.

"Come on!" he protested. "That was a good one!"

"How long've you been sitting on that for?"

He didn't answer, which usually meant he'd been waiting to tell his joke for quite some time. Knowing him, he'd come up with it the minute I'd

11

joined our uni's cycling society, all the way back in October.

Overall, the first afternoon was decent. Dan had a bunch of plans, but I insisted we take the leaflets back to the cottage and make Matt go through them with us. He'd only woken up a few minutes before we got back, and was already complaining about being hungry.

"You can't be hungry already," Dan said, helping me pack the groceries away. "You haven't done anything all day."

"Slept through lunch, didn't I? Kyle, can you get me something? I'm dying here."

I offered the most dramatic sigh I could muster and informed him all I would make was toast.

"You're an angel."

"Yeah, yeah."

The rain cleared up, and the sun returned to us the next day. We took the day to explore the village; just something light and easy. I spent as long as I could in the museum (to avoid following Dan into every last corner of every book and charity shop), and Matt was content to spend the morning looking around a souvenir shop. Dan bought so much tat, I wasn't sure how he was going to get it all home. He wasn't impressed when I told him he'd need a second suitcase.

The day after that, Dan wanted to do nothing so his bank account could recover. This seemed like the perfect time to take on my role as wingman. I said I was going on a cycle trail, intending to leave Matt and Dan alone for the day. Matt decided he wanted to go, though, so I adjusted my plans and we packed ourselves a picnic lunch.

Dan had been right about the bike. Mine was fairly new since I'd only taken up cycling a few months ago, but Matt's bike was visibly rusting and creaked when he wheeled it out of the laundry room.

I'm not cruel. I asked if Matt was sure about the trail we'd picked. He said he was.

It was unbearably hot even before we started up the steep incline of the hill. Some of this was our own fault: I was trying to shift some depression weight at the time, and I'd thrown on a dark shirt for the day. I'd been hoping it wouldn't turn see-through if (when) I started to sweat in it. Matt had never left his emo phase, so he was in all black and grey at the time as well. He was in much better shape than me, but he was struggling to make his weird old bike move.

Now, most of the time in the UK, it's raining, it's freezing, or it's both. This wouldn't be a problem, except that it was neither on this fine day. The sun was beating down with an absolute vengeance, and I felt just a little as if I was dying. Judging by his laboured breathing, Matt was having an equally bad time.

It took forever to reach the top of the hill. I was sure we'd just cycled through hell by mistake.

Anyway, at the very top of the hill was a small picnic area overlooking the countryside. I propped my bike against the single table and promptly downed half the contents of my water bottle.

Matt tried to do the same thing and the chain immediately fell off his bike. It must have been loose already, because it clattered quietly and fell into the grass. He blinked down at it with a look that said *I'm not mad, just disappointed.*

"S'pose it's been a long time coming," he said. I nodded.

"A moment of silence for our fallen comrade."

Matt gave me an unamused look. It was worth it.

Had I actually seen Matt's eyes before? It was hard to say. His dark brown hair was arranged in the standard emo cut, with his fringe falling down over his eyes. It was normally quite fluffy, but the hot weather and hard work meant sweat had flattened it against his forehead. I wasn't doing much better, mind you.

"Look, let's have lunch, and we'll walk back together," I said. "I'm not leaving you stranded at the top of this hill." The hill felt more like a mountain anyway. I was eager not to descend alone.

"Yeah. Okay."

"Want me to call Dan to come rescue us?"

"No, no… it's not like he has a bike I could borrow or anything."

"Well, if he did, I'm sure you'd be allowed to sit on the back of it."

Matt went quiet and I couldn't tell if that was a good sign or not.

Neither of us was thrilled about having to walk back when it was scorching, so we took our time with lunch. I wished I knew what to say to make either of us feel better. Matt probably felt the same. Instead of thinking about that, we sat at the picnic bench and stared out over the hills. We could see Broadway Tower from where we were, and I suggested we take Dan up to the tower and leave him there. That earned me a small smile from Matt.

"He wouldn't leave even if we tried to make him."

"You say that like it's a bad thing."

"I mean, he can cook more than toast and ping dinners."

"And here I thought you liked him."

Silence again.

At last, Matt stood up and announced we'd better start heading back. I'd purposely left making the call up to him, considering he was going to have the hardest time. I did offer to swap bikes so he could go on ahead, which he seriously considered for a couple of minutes but, ultimately, we resolved to walk back together. That way, neither of us had to suffer alone.

Somehow, going down the hill took significantly longer than going up. I supposed we *had* been cycling up the hill, and it was much more difficult trying not to let gravity take over so we didn't fall the whole way down. At some point we discovered we'd lost the trail, and it was now too late (and far too hot) to turn back.

Rex Alistair

Quite a bit of swearing was done and we had to stop so Matt could check our location on his phone.

He huffed a lot. Everything was my fault now.

"Yes," I said. "I lost the trail on purpose. So sorry I'm not a human compass."

"Know what, Kyle, just shut up for a minute so I can read the map, alright?"

Matt glowered at his phone while I sat on the side of the road and discovered that it was, in fact, possible to drink water aggressively. *Maybe that can be my new party trick*, I thought.

"Right," Matt said, pointing behind us and off to the right. "It's that way. Come on."

"Are you sure?" I asked. He was pointing uphill. "Maybe we should keep heading downhill and—"

"No."

"Matt, come on—"

"You got us lost. The map says this is the quickest way back. We're going this way."

I relented, but I wasn't happy about it. We marched on in tense silence, unsure who to be more mad at: ourselves or each other. It was simply too hot to argue anymore. I was out of water, and Matt soon ran out as well. *He'd better not complain about it*, I thought. If he did, I was going to point out that we could be in a town by now—one with shops and cafés and *water*—if we'd gone down the damn hill. Instead, here I was, mouth drier than paper, skin burning, lungs on fire. If

Matt tried to use the shower first, I'd throw him in the back garden and turn the hose on him.

We would definitely be late getting back. *Very* late. If we were lucky, Dan wasn't already calling the police in a blind panic. He watched too much true crime, and I think he forgot we could take care of ourselves.

Then again, we were lost and ready to drop from exposure in a country whose biggest area of unexplored wilderness is the Cadbury factory. Outside of heatwaves, I had to tie my house key onto my hoodie so I didn't lose it. Matt had to wear Velcro shoes because he couldn't tie his laces properly.

Most of the time, though, we could take care of ourselves.

If Dan was trying to call the police right now instead of me or Matt, I'd throw him in the garden and hose *him* down as well.

"Hey," Matt panted, stopping so abruptly that I almost fell over his bike. "Is that what I think it is?"

Matt was pointing down the hill now. Just off the road, trying to hide amidst a fairly large patch of overgrown grass, was a small building made from gold brick. It looked like a tiny barn with a chimney, and climbing ivy encircled the windows and door. There was a sign above the door which read, in neat, hand-painted white text: 4TH TIME LUCKY.

I exchanged a look with Matt.

"Looks like a pub," I said.

"Could be. They must have water."

We made our way over and propped our bikes under the window. I couldn't see a thing past the climbing ivy, and there was only the smoke coming from the chimney to indicate it might be open. Matt pushed on the door. It was old-fashioned and made of heavy wood, and the metal parts—the hinges, the handle, even the lock on the front—seemed to be made of brass. They were styled to look like old iron, but they were definitely brass.

When we stepped inside, we discovered it was not a pub but a tearoom. There were people chattering away inside and a fire was crackling merrily in the back corner. We found an empty table by the window, which was letting in plenty of light despite being covered by ivy. Our table was small and the wooden chairs creaked when we sat, but we were a little more comfortable. My feet had been aching a while now and it was just a relief to be seated.

The fire made the tearoom feel warm, but not hot or stuffy, and it smelled comforting and familiar. I felt just a little hazy and it made me think of Saturday mornings with my dad.

"God, it smells nice in here," Matt said, picking up a menu and examining it. The menus were written on what seemed to be parchment, and were entirely handwritten in black ink. There were little spots where the ink had dripped onto the paper. *The owner must be a bit eccentric*, I thought.

"Got your wallet?" I asked. My stomach was starting to growl and I'd barely glanced at the menu. "I think I'm going to eat."

"Yeah, same actually."

A waitress appeared from the back, probably where the kitchen was. She was pale, blonde, and wore all black except for the purple-striped apron about her waist and the silver necklace with a purple jewel set into it. Her earrings glinted as she passed the fire.

"Matt, Kyle," she said, "welcome. What do you need?"

We ordered, and before she could leave, I said, "Can you fill our bottles up? Please?"

The waitress nodded and took our bottles into the back. It was only then that I realised what a strange question she'd asked us. Not *what would you like*; not *what can I get you*. She'd said *what do you need?*

Maybe we just looked desperate or something. I wouldn't have been surprised.

I took the time to look around as we waited. The walls were all cluttered like a Ghibli movie: wooden shelves had been stuffed to bursting with decorative plates and China teapots and figurines, which seemed to have come from every place imaginable. It was the patrons, though, who really caught my attention.

The tearoom was serving all sorts of people, which made sense to me, except that there were people talking who I never would have expected to see coexisting so comfortably in the same place. The main two who surprised me were a man in bright shorts, who had a gay pride flag tied around his shoulders like a cape, and a man in sweatpants and trainers, who looked like the sort of person you'd expect to have about four teeth. They were talking so loudly, I couldn't help overhearing them.

From what I could make out, the guy in sweatpants was due to become a father, and he was excited but woefully underprepared. He was venting to the guy wearing the pride flag, and his eyes were all red and puffy. After a moment, I realised his voice was still rough.

"I just don't know how I'm s'pose to support them," he lamented. "I can't leave her an' that little babby on their own, but I can't even afford a pram or nuffin."

The guy in the pride flag pulled up something on his phone and showed it to the guy in the sweatpants, saying, "My sister has this. One wheel's come off so she's getting rid for cheap. Should be an easy fix."

Sweatpants guy scrutinized whatever pride flag man was showing him and said, "That's perfect. You sure it'd be okay?"

"Oh, aye. Sounds like you need it. Here—"

The waitress came back then, and I lost track of their conversation. I hadn't realised how hungry I was until I looked up thirty seconds later and discovered my whole sandwich was gone.

"You actually taste that?" Matt asked. He was smirking a little bit.

"Maybe," I said. "We'll never know."

"*I'll* never know."

"Neither of us."

Matt snorted. I don't remember if I did taste the food, but I do remember feeling very satisfied afterwards. Occasionally I wonder if it was so good because I was hungry, or for another reason. I've never quite figured it out.

We ate in silence—or rather, Matt ate while I sipped my iced tea—and the waitress bustled about, cleaning tables and serving other customers. I watched the guy in the sweatpants and the man in the pride flag continue to talk for a while, before the man in the pride flag stood up.

"Right," he said. "Best be off. You gonna be okay if I leave you here?"

"I'll be fine, mate. Go have fun at Pride."

This threw me off. We'd looked it up while planning our holiday, and there were no Pride events nearby for at least a couple more months. Moreover, it was too late now if the man planned to drive to an event. Everybody would be in the process of packing up by the time he got there. As I turned to Matt, the waitress approached a stand near the front. There was a Victorian-looking cash register on it. She handed the man his change and said:

"Thanks for stopping by, Kevin. We look forward to seeing you again."

Pride Flag Man paused, shifting his weight to one leg and leaning heavily on it. "Oh, er—thanks," he said, "but I've had my three visits. Better not risk it."

The waitress gave him a strange smile. "I understand. Have a good afternoon."

The man nodded and left. Matt and I glanced at one another, but I couldn't tell if he found any of it as weird as I did.

We stayed a while longer, until we felt ready to try heading back again. The guy in the sweatpants looked up as I stood to leave. We accidentally made eye contact, both did that awkward White Person Smile, and turned away from each other. Matt and I paid and left.

It was significantly cooler outside, and Matt was visibly happier. I was feeling better, too, come to think of it.

"We should bring Dan here," Matt said as we picked up our bikes. "I reckon he'd love it."

I agreed. We spent the rest of the holiday allowing Dan to drag us around various places— Broadway Tower, an enchanted forest, the steam train and the other villages it ran to—and on the last day, we decided to take him to the tearoom.

Matt was sure we were lost at first, but I recognised the patch of overgrown grass.

"You guys," Dan said, "are not very funny. Why didn't you just tell me you wanted to go exploring?"

The barn-shaped building was there. Still small and gold-brick; still covered in climbing ivy. There was no neatly painted sign, however, and the ivy had died a long time ago. The windows were all broken and the door was off its hinges. Matt scowled and we followed him inside. The building was dark and empty, nothing but dirt occupying a single room which was a completely different shape to the one we'd spent part of our afternoon in just a few days prior.

Rex Alistair

The second time, you will want it.

September rolled around and we went back to uni. I moved into a new house with Dan, one where I wouldn't have to wear three jumpers in the winter, and Matt spent so much time with us that people thought he'd moved in. This was obviously because he loved us so much, and not because his own housemates were absolute nightmares (one was a party animal and the other was never quiet and awake at the same time). At some point—I think it was just before Halloween—we started cooking together on Saturdays and then having game nights after dinner.

The first time we did this, I managed to blow up a bowl of gravy in the microwave.

"God, you're a mess," Matt told me, sounding an awful lot like my mother. "I'm surprised you've made it past childhood."

I was trying to save what I could of the gravy and didn't respond.

The local museum and university library became my second and third homes, albeit not in that order. They were invaluable resources for my dissertation, and the library had access to coffee almost twenty-four hours a day. I was also on our Cycling Society's committee, which probably involved a lot less teamwork than it really should. I've always been convinced the problem was down to Mark.

Mark took his role as society president a wee bit too seriously, but not in a way that was particularly helpful. The rest of us had started calling him our *Glorious Leader* when he wasn't around. Mark's universe revolved specifically around Mark, and nobody else.

Nobody except for Rachel, at least. Rachel was short, sweet, and brunette, and Mark hated me because I worked in the library with her a couple of times a week. We liked to get in a couple of hours once classes—or the Tuesday committee meeting—were done for the day, and our schedules lined up pretty well. We would often set up in a quiet corner, or an empty study room if we were lucky, and spend about an hour studying. Then one of us would complain of being hungry or thirsty or sore or tired, so we'd pack up and spend the next hour in the library café. At some point, the friendly conversation would devolve into every Brit's favourite pastime: complaining. At some point after *that,* the conversation would usually turn to complaining about Mark.

See, Mark had a thing for Rachel, and everybody knew it. Especially Rachel. She also happened to have a long-term boyfriend and wouldn't be interested in Mark even if she didn't. Apparently her boyfriend, Dave, thought it was funny. He complained about Mark a lot too.

"I just wish," Rachel lamented one rainy evening in late October, "the rest of the committee would shut him up for once. I've been trying to get him thinking about For Change since August."

For Change was a charity event Cycle Soc ran annually, full music and live performances, where attendees were encouraged to donate as much change as they could. Rachel, being Cycle Soc's secretary, had a ton of work to do to get it up and running. Most of that work needed to be done in advance, and she needed approval from the rest of the committee before she could get started. Mark took over the meetings entirely, though, and wouldn't talk about it because Rachel wouldn't date him.

I sipped my hot chocolate and said, "We'll bring it up in the next meeting."

"I've been trying. Weren't you paying attention?"

Honestly, I'd been doodling a Roman coin in my notebook. I cleared my throat and said, "We could double-team him."

Rachel snorted.

"No, really," I said. "If we can take over the others will help us gang up on him. Then he'll have to think about it."

"*If.*"

I conceded, but decided I would come up with a way to force Mark and the others into planning For Change. While the conversation moved on, I watched the poor café workers mutter to one another not to bother telling people about the sign on the door anymore, and then I watched people bump into the door when it didn't open automatically for them. For the record, the sign read **DOOR LOCKED DUE TO BAD WEATHER. PLEASE USE SIDE ENTRANCE.** It was a nice, big sign. Bold letters. Very visible. A surprising number of people missed it. Rachel, facing away from the door, heard the occasional *thump* and saw me trying not to crack up.

"Glad you're entertained."

"I'm just picturing Mark flying into the window like a pigeon," I said. Rachel let out a small laugh.

"We'd all love to see it."

"I don't know about you, but I'd pay to see it. Maybe we should put him through a window at For Change."

"I mean, does it count as murder if it's for entertainment?"

"I think you'll find public executions used to be very common."

"Oh, how silly of me," Rachel said. "I forgot you were a history professor."

"Not yet, but I *do* know everything." I took a bite out of the cupcake I'd bought to go with my hot chocolate. There was another wet *thump* from the automatic door.

The cupcake gave me—if I may say so—a rather brilliant idea. On Monday, I emailed my lecturers to pull a sickie, asked Matt and Dan for their help when classes were over, and cracked open one of Dan's bakery books.

It took two days to finish cleaning the kitchen, but it was absolutely worth it.

On Tuesday, I rolled into the meeting carrying three cake tins. They were filled with the things I'd baked (with a lot of help from Dan) the day before. Honestly, the ones I'd had help with turned out the best. Dan's always had a habit of stress baking, and he was perpetually stressed during university, so he'd gotten very good at it.

I was the last one into the meeting room, so I already had everyone's attention. All I had to do from there was place the tins in the middle of the table and remove their lids.

"Are those for us?" Rachel asked, reaching for a somewhat malformed bit of shortbread I'd attempted to make.

I nodded. "Made them yesterday. Figured I'd try a few things, see what we want to do at For Change."

Mark didn't look at me. "That's months off. We don't need to worry about it yet."

"We've got a lot of prep work to do," I said. "Might as well get the fiddly bits out the way."

Relief was visible on Rachel's face as the rest of the committee agreed. Mark was less than pleased, but I managed to railroad the meeting so that we actually got somewhere with the preparations. In the library later, Rachel told me she felt like a weight had lifted from her shoulders, which was exactly what I'd been hoping for.

Now we had a list of venues to look at, and a set of charities to consider donating money to, all we had to do was put everything else together.

"Mark's really petty," Rachel pointed out. "He's gonna make your life hell if he can."

"I know. I'll be fine."

For a couple of months, I was right. Mark made me do as much as he could, but I was able to hold out until March which, in retrospect, is actually quite impressive. March had been a rough time for three years at this point, so I already was in… not the best place. It was also the time I had to *really* start worrying about my dissertation and other work. Combine that with everything Mark had me doing, and I have to say I've definitely been better. I was struggling to get more than a couple hours of sleep at a time, too, so I probably looked a mess on top of feeling like one. Rachel had been helping quite a bit with the For Change preparations, but we were the only two really doing anything. This was manageable until her father suddenly fell very ill.

Knowing exactly how Rachel was feeling, I instructed her to go home and be with her family. She asked Dave to take over her part of the work, and he really did his best, but he had no idea what he was doing, so I had to correct a lot of it.

I suppose Mark didn't like me sending his unrequited crush away, because he suddenly decided— five weeks before the event, mind you—that he didn't like the charity we'd picked. We simply *had* to interview three new charities immediately. Of course, he'd thoughtfully set it all up, and it just so happened that I was the only one available to talk to them. It would be easy enough, he claimed. All I had to do was meet with the representatives, chat a bit about what we did and what the charities did, and ask what they planned to do with the money. Then I'd report back, and we'd all pick a charity together.

Mark was probably going to change his mind afterwards and go with the original charity, but I was too out of it to argue. I went along to the interviews like the dutiful dummy I was.

The first two meetings weren't so bad, except that nobody told me I had my jumper on inside out. I also felt like my heart was going to explode because I'd chased down two caffeine pills with an energy drink *and* a cup of coffee that morning.

Pro tip: don't do that. You can and will spend the whole day wondering if you're about to become the youngest person in your city to die of a heart attack.

Anyway, I arrived early to the third meeting, jumper on properly now, blissfully unaware that I was about to spend the next thirty minutes talking to the human equivalent of a headache.

I was about five minutes early to the meeting, I think. It took so long to get buzzed into the building that I wound up being almost ten minutes late.

The first thing I noticed about Paul was his highlighter-yellow flip-flops. I didn't want to judge on appearance alone, but did he really think I wasn't even worth a pair of ratty old trainers? Call me judgemental, but it bothered me. After being offered a handshake like a dead fish, I knew I didn't want to give Paul a single penny. Still, I'd agreed to the meeting, and I didn't want to go back to crying over my dissertation just yet, so I powered through.

I firmly believe Paul was a politician in a past life. He was so good at talking in circles (and I was so bloody exhausted) that it took me a while to realise what he was doing. I stopped him and asked what the fundraiser money would be going towards. Then I had to do it three more times. At last, I got fed up.

"Paul," I said, cutting off the fifth or sixth circle, "I'm sorry, mate, but I *need* to know what you're doing with this money or I won't be able to give you anything."

He faltered. "We-*ell*," he began, slowly, "the way we work, you see—we have this pot that we take money out for—"

"Yeah, you've said. That doesn't answer my question."

"So, for example, it'll go into the pot and—"

"Paul. I need an actual answer." I knew I was getting snippy with him, but I was tired, my head was banging, and I wanted to go with the first charity I'd spoken to anyway. More importantly, I wanted to get out of there and have a power nap before dinner.

"Well, I can't give you one now because—"

"Okay, thanks for your time."

I left the building, found a bench, and sat down to update the rest of the committee. Mark tried to give me grief for walking out. I wasn't in the mood and gave

31

it right back. He was the one who changed his mind about the charity at the last minute, I pointed out; he should have been the one meeting with the potential new ones. Then I switched my phone off so I wouldn't have to deal with him for a while.

I'd love to say something like *Ah, blessed silence*, but the background noise of the city was suddenly much, *much* louder. Car engines rumbled, people shouted and laughed, busses hissed as they went on their way, and all of it was pressing in on me. If I didn't look at the people walking past, they could pretend they didn't see me trying not to cry while I glared at my blank phone screen.

I don't know how long I sat there. I *do* know I snapped out of it when a woman crouched in front of me. She wore a puffy silver jacket, tank top and skinny jeans, and her hair was scraped back into a ponytail.

"You alright, bab?" the woman asked. "Need a Curly Wurly?"

I shook my head. Now I thought about it, I did feel a bit off—my blood sugar was probably getting low—but I wasn't about to tell a stranger that.

"That's okay, bab. What d'you need?"

I shook my head again. I couldn't find my voice to tell her I'd be fine as long as I was left alone. I just needed to cry the stress out for a while.

"Sure you're alright, mate?"

The second voice made me look up, because I recognised it. It was the guy in the sweatpants, from that strange tearoom outside Broadway. He wore jeans now, and nice shoes. He was pushing a pram with a single hot pink wheel, and a look in his eye told me he recognised me. He paused for a moment, thinking, then pushed the pram toward the woman. The baby in the pram kicked its little legs and yelled, "Ma!"

"I'll look after 'im, Hail," he said. "Catch y'up later. You take care of Penny."

The woman looked uncertain, but she kissed the man on the cheek and began pushing the pram away.

"Right," he said. "Name's Ryan. What's yours?"

I told him. My throat felt thick, and my voice was rough and wet.

"Kyle," he said carefully, "d'you want to go back to that tearoom?"

I found that I did. Even though Matt and I had nearly killed each other that day, the thought of the weird fire and the overstuffed walls and the bizarre mishmash of patrons was comforting.

"But it's in the Cotswolds," I pointed out. Ryan opened his mouth to say something that looked like it was going to be snarky, but stopped himself.

"Fair play. Come on, let's get you a hot drink. My treat."

He let me get up on my own, and matched my pace as he guided me through the streets to a café I hadn't seen in the city before. The outside looked the same as every other building on the street, except that I couldn't see through the windows, the door was made of heavy wood and brass, and the sign over the door read 4ᵀᴴ TIME LUCKY.

It was the tearoom.

Sure, you might be thinking, they could have branched out. Perhaps they'd even moved, except that then the interior and staff should be different. Ryan hesitated in the doorway, gesturing for me to go in first. Everything was exactly the same, right down to the ugly red rug on the dark wood floor and the rectangular shape of the room. Even the strange fire still reminded me of my dad. The exact same waitress greeted us, too.

"Kyle," she said, "Ryan. Welcome back. It's nice to see you again."

"Same t'you duck," Ryan said, guiding me into a chair. He murmured something I didn't hear, then sat next to me as the waitress headed to the back. When she brought over our drinks, Ryan said, "Right. Tell me what's up."

I opened my mouth and everything burst out. The anniversary of my father's death; the lack of sleep and excess of uni work; Mark making me run For Change virtually by myself; the rest of the committee (except Rachel and Dave, but he wasn't on the committee) just *letting* him. I didn't mean to tell Ryan everything, but it was impossible to stop. Ryan asked the waitress for some paper and a pen. She ripped a page out of her notebook and fished a pen out of her apron pocket. He started making notes. When I was done, he flipped the page over to the blank side and said:

"Right. Sounds to me like y'need to make some free time. Ever heard of the spoons theory?"

"Um… no."

Ryan explained, in more detail and using actual spoons, that the spoons theory is about how much energy a person has to do certain tasks. Case in point: you *could* lift a sugar cube with one spoon, but it was generally easier to use two. He said it sounded like I had too many tasks and not enough spoons. Unfortunately, this made an awful lot of sense.

Please don't ask me why but Ryan always used two spoons to lift his sugar cubes. Apparently it was just a thing he did.

We formulated a plan. I was going to tell the committee I wanted to go with the first charity, and then I'd inform them I needed to take a step back for my mental health. This was going to be non-negotiable, Ryan said. For Change was not my problem anymore.

He paid for both our drinks, and I felt a hell of a lot better as we got up to leave. He gave me his phone number with instructions to call him when I got home, or if I needed anything.

"Congratulations, Ryan," the waitress said as we left. "You've been lucky."

"So's the kid. Nice knowing you, duck."

"We'll certainly miss you," the waitress said. I thought she sounded a little sad.

Rex Alistair

The third time, you will ask for it.

Things improved after we left. I still felt a bit rough, so Ryan insisted I go for a walk and then call him when I got home, even if it was three in the morning. Admittedly, I was tempted to find a secluded spot and sit there until I had to go home… but the more I thought about it, the more I wanted to go to bed and take a long nap. That sounded especially appealing when the weather took a turn.

Remember how Britain is always raining, freezing, or both? Well, the weather doesn't get bad; it gets *nasty*. The rain is sharp and cold and is accompanied by a wind so vicious you have to peel your sodden clothes off your wet skin when you get home, even with a raincoat and umbrella.

I didn't have a raincoat or umbrella. I also—and I only discovered this when my socks started squelching—didn't have waterproof shoes.

This meant that, as well as my jumper and jeans and everything underneath, I would have to wring out my *socks* before I could warm up in the shower. Lovely.

Still, a nap in some dry clothes did make me feel better. Only then did I remember I was supposed to call Ryan. He picked up on the second ring.

"Hello? Get back alright, kid? Bit wet?"

"Housemate says I look like a drowned rat."

Ryan had a laugh like a dog barking—short and loud and rough. He always laughed very hard, even when he wasn't laughing at something very funny.

"I bet," he said, when he was done laughing. "How you feeling now?"

"Better," I admitted, although I was sure I'd feel worse again when I checked my messages.

"Have some soup, yeah? With a bit of bread and butter. Really nice when it's raining out."

"Sure."

Ryan paused, then said, "Listen, I know you've got uni work and your cycling club and all that, but I wanna invite you out some time. Me and some mates play poker down our local on Friday nights. You should join us."

I didn't know what to say other than, "I haven't played poker before. I don't know how."

"We can teach you. No pressure, mind, but the first drink's free."

Well, how could I say no to that? Ryan's local was about a ten-minute walk from my house. It was busy and loud, but I sort of knew Ryan, and his friends were really cool. I think he knew them from work. One of them, a huge bloke with a phenomenal beard, turned out to be the man in the pride flag. His name was Kevin. He'd only just met Ryan on the day of my first visit to the 4th Time Lucky but, like me, he'd been pulled into Ryan's friendship group. I didn't know if Kevin recognised me, but he was friendly and let me team up with him because I hadn't played poker before.

I was quite terrible.

"Don't worry about it," he said as I apologised for the umpteenth time for losing all his money. "You'll get the hang of it—just takes practise."

Still, I had fun, even if I had no idea what I was doing and wanted to learn for next time. Considering Ryan had helped me organise my time better, I now had time to learn, although Mark had been disappointed to find out how I'd made so much time for myself. Or, rather, how Ryan had helped me make so much time for myself.

Ryan essentially worked as a human calendar for an entire office. He was extremely good at it, and had worked his magic on organising For Change for the low, low price of owing him a couple of drinks some time. Furious with the committee for being lazy as hell even though I had more work to do than the rest of them combined, I'd agreed to let Ryan draw up a schedule.

Under Ryan's instruction, I sent them the organisation timetable and announced that I'd be sticking to it exactly, so they all needed to do the same. I had to focus on my coursework, after all, and could absolutely *not* take on any extra work right now. If that meant For Change suffered because none of them wanted to do their share of the work, so be it. Ryan had made me swear I wouldn't let anyone trick me into taking on extra work. He was right; it wasn't fair that I should be doing the whole thing by myself.

Mark tried to argue, and I'm proud to say I told him off for it. How dare he, the Glorious Leader of Cycle Soc, try to shirk everything off on me? Why were the others just letting him?

Nobody had a good answer for me. I told them I would be stepping down from the committee the second For Change was over, on the grounds that their lack of teamwork was exhausting to deal with, then put the group chat on mute and asked Rachel if she and Dave wanted to join me, Matt, and Dan for a game night when she got back to uni. She said she'd be back next week and they'd love to come along.

I had officially upgraded myself to a fifth wheel. *Oops.*

In the meantime, now that I was actually free to do so, I finally finished my dissertation and started doing things for myself again. Mark tried to complain that he couldn't handle his two organisational tasks. I told him to pull his fingers out and get the others to do the same. Then, pumped from adrenaline, I applied for a weekend job at the city museum. They offered me ten hours a week and Ryan's wife invited me out for brunch to celebrate. I took Rachel with me, to take her mind off what was happening at home. She seemed relieved to be out of the house.

Brunch was nice, and Rachel's father was on the mend so she was looking miles brighter. She actually *laughed* when Ryan made me recount the tantrums Mark had been throwing. Rachel later told me she got the impression Ryan wanted to give Mark a smack, and I told her he would absolutely love to but I thought it would be an unfair fight.

"How did you two meet?" Rachel asked, towards the end of brunch. Ryan and I blinked at each other, unsure what we should tell her. *Actually we met in Howl's Moving Tearoom and I'd like to show you but so far it's turned into an abandoned barn and then a charity shop?* No; I'd sound crazy.

"Uh—we met on holiday," I said. "Then Ryan wanted to help with For Change."

Ryan nodded. "Reckon Kyle should give me a free ticket, actually."

"I'll think about it."

"You can buy me a ticket too, if you want," Rachel said.

"You've got a boyfriend."

"Buy him one as well."

"Like a date? Don't go putting ideas in Mark's head."

Ryan let out a long, loud snort. Then he did his barking laugh. He really did love it when we bullied Mark. Rachel, who'd been happy but awkward for most of the meal, also laughed. I was pleased to hear it; her laugh was slightly obnoxious and very infectious. It lightened the mood immediately.

Rachel and I were supposed to go to the library after brunch so she could catch up on her coursework, since she was behind and I was nearly finished. Of course, it would end the same as it always did: with us complaining about anything and everything for an hour. I told her to go on ahead and find us a good spot. I said I needed a word with Ryan, so I'd catch her up.

When we were alone, Ryan asked what was up.

"How come you didn't tell Rachel about the tearoom?" Ryan shrugged, and I added, "Have you told Hailey?"

"Of course not! You ever told anyone?"

The truth was, except for telling Dan we'd found a nice place he'd really love, I hadn't. I'd never even discussed it with Matt after we'd left Broadway, let alone told him I'd been there a second time. It had just never felt right to tell him. What I couldn't understand was *why* it hadn't felt right to tell him.

"It isn't normal not to talk about that place," I said, "is it?"

"Definitely not."

"Then… why?"

"Search me," Ryan said, with another shrug. "Just one of those things. Like… what's the fire smell like to you?"

Cinnamon with just a hint of chlorine. "My dad's favourite doughnuts," I said. "We used to go swimming then get them for lunch."

"See, to me, it smells like the seaside."

"What?"

41

Rex Alistair

It hadn't occurred to me before that something about the fire should be off. It was strange, sure, but to smell different to different people... what did that *mean*? For a moment, I thought about asking Matt what the fire had smelled like to him, but a part of me instinctively decided against it. Maybe it just wasn't something you asked a person who'd only been there once.

"Used to love the sea as a kid, so it smells like the seaside, y'know?"

"You seem to know a lot about this."

"Can't say I'm the full authority. You should check out QuestionEverything, though. They talk about it a lot—might give you some answers, yeah?"

"Answers you can't give me?"

Ryan answered, unsurprisingly, with another shrug. I went to help Rachel, and pulled up QuestionEverything when I got home. It was an ugly forum-hosting website, full of alien hunters and Illuminati-fearing conspiracy theorists. Despite this, I was able to find a forum about the 4th Time Lucky. A forum which, it seemed, was occupied exclusively by people who'd been there before.

It turned out the tearoom's patrons came from all over the globe. I only spoke English—unless you count looking up swear words in my Year Nine Spanish class—but I could see all sorts of languages were being used. So then, it wasn't restricted to England, America, and whichever other countries spoke mainly English.

What the hell was going on? I'd been half expecting alien theories, but they were nowhere to be found.

Well, one person thought aliens might be involved, but everyone else laughed him out of the thread. What would aliens get out of running a tearoom? They didn't need our money and it was a totally nonsensical way to study us. That was a fair point, but the other theories seemed equally unlikely to me. Ghosts and government spies were the ideas with the most traction, but I doubted them both. Government spies could absolutely not be the same person every time, and if ghosts were involved, then this was a *very* unique case that Dave would have told me about months ago.

I leaned back, unsatisfied. All I could really gather was that the waitress was the same every time, and she was fluent in every language she encountered.

Perhaps, if Ryan hadn't been so eager to help before, I would have ignored the whole thing. He gave me the impression there was more here than conspiracy theories, though, so I persisted.

It took some time, but I eventually noticed there were an awful lot of comments popping up from an account called *thewaitress*. As far as I could tell, all this account did was respond to conspiracy theories with either a wink or a smiley face. I clicked on the username, expecting to find a full list of comments—if you can really call winky and smiley faces comments—but instead I was met with dead air. Nothing loaded, no matter what I did. Refreshing the page; backtracking and trying again; even resetting the Wi-Fi didn't work.

Rex Alistair

Damn it. It could take hours to trawl through the forum and find what I was looking for. I resolved to give it half an hour, but soon remembered I could simply set the comments from oldest to newest.

The very first comment in the forum, the one which had started it off, was from *thewaitress*.

The first time, you will need it.

The second time, you will want it.

The third time, you will ask for it.

The fourth time, you must be very, very lucky.

There is no fifth time.

Some of this made sense right off the bat. 'It', obviously, referred to the tearoom. The tearoom had appeared when Matt and I needed a place to rest before we killed each other; it had reappeared when I'd wanted everything in my life to stop for a few minutes so I could catch up. *There is no fifth time...* that had to mean a person could only make four visits. Kevin had said something about that when I'd first seen him, I was sure.

So, then, what did the rest mean? How was I supposed to ask for it? Why did I need to be lucky?

Surely there was a set of instructions somewhere. A guide to summoning the tearoom. I made myself an account and clicked on *thewaitress*'s username again.

This time, I was met with a small text box and the words, *Send them a message!*

Ah—now I was getting somewhere. I introduced myself and then wrote:

> *I've been to the 4th Time Lucky twice now.*
> *Will I find out more if I ask for it?*
> *Also, how do I ask for it?*

Not the most interesting message, but I'd cut out a significant amount of rambling.

I sent the message, and promptly forgot about it on the grounds that I had other things to do. The next three days were uninteresting. On the third day, though, I got a text from an unknown number. Usually, I'd ignore those—I got a lot of scam texts at the time—but this one was different. Instead of the name of some bank I didn't actually use, there was simply a blank space. Not even a phone number. I decided to open the message.

Rex Alistair

Hi Kyle,

to ask for the Tea Room, you can either travel to its home in Scotland, or you can summon it. If summoning is easier, you'll need a summoning spell and a place you won't be distracted, with a door. The best time for this is duck.

Good luck!

There was no name attached, but I could guess who it was from. As I was reading, a second text came through from the same number.

Dusk, not duck. Sorry!

Ah, that made sense. I didn't have a spell book, and there were no summoning spells on QuestionEverything, so my next option was to search online and hope for the best. There were plenty of different spells out there, some serious and some... less serious. The good news was that I already had a place in mind; somewhere I wouldn't look like an idiot if the spell didn't work. Somewhere that made you want to believe in magic. All I needed to do now was pick the right spell and gather my ingredients.

Just on the outskirts of my city, there was a huge park full of hills and wildflowers. I'm not sure it even counted as a park, it was so enormous. People rarely went there outside daylight hours, so it was perfect for what I was doing.

The waitress had said I needed a door. There was a gate in the park, but what I really had in mind was an enormous, old tree on the side of a hill. People played around it all day, and I'd seen folks heftier than me clambering between the overhanging roots and into the hollow in the trunk. It was a little dramatic, but I liked it, and I didn't want to set off the smoke alarm in my room. The day before For Change, I packed all the spell ingredients into my backpack and cycled out to the park.

The big, old tree looked creepy in the fading daylight. Looming above me with the sun behind it and the shadows lengthening, the patterns in its bark formed a shape that looked an awful lot like a face. The face watched on, leering in amusement as I emptied my backpack.

I had brought a handful of dried plants with me—rosemary, thyme, violets—all bundled up in hawthorn sticks and tied up with string. I struck a match and lit the bundle as the rose gold of sunset began to fade from the sky.

Immediately, a great plume of thick, dark smoke billowed up from the centre of the bundle. The smell coming from it was sickly and so overwhelming, my nose started to burn and my eyes began to water. Blearily, through the curtain of smoke and my half-closed eyes, I could make out the shape of the tree.

Rex Alistair

It looked like it was breathing.

It looked like the roots were on fire.

It looked like the frowny face was screaming.

I could swear I heard the branches crack and creak, as though an unseen force was pulling them about and forcing them into new, unnatural positions.

The bundle gave a fizzling *pop!* and dwindled rapidly into soot, which got up my nose and made me sneeze.

Nothing seemed to have changed, and I'll be the first to admit I was disappointed. Had I done something wrong? I could have sworn it was working while the bundle was lit. I thought perhaps I'd made a mistake, but my ingredients had disintegrated, so I couldn't simply try again. It would have to be back to the drawing board for now, I supposed.

I turned to go, and that was when the tree began to creak and groan again. Whirling around to face it, I discovered something had indeed changed: the roots had moved. They formed an archway just big enough to crawl through. I'd expected the hollow to form the doorway, but this would do.

So crawl through I did, for a very long time. Far longer than I realistically should have.

The dirt under me was loose and soft, freshly disturbed, but the roots forming the rest of the tunnel were hard and dry, as though they hadn't moved in a very long time. The tunnel sloped gently downwards, into the hill, and I could see much better than you might expect. There was something bioluminescent in the roots, in the dirt, in the *air*. It glowed a faint blue as I crawled past. I couldn't see the end of the tunnel, but I could see enough to know where I was going.

As it turned out, I couldn't see the end because there was nothing to make it glow. I know this because I went face-first into it, squashing my nose and probably looking very cartoonish in the process.

Actually, I fell a couple of feet and landed on my face, discovering the hard way that the tunnel had abruptly widened out in all directions. I'm fairly sure I landed in a scorpion pose.

There was enough room to stand up now—which I did—but not at all enough room to move about. It felt like I was standing in a wardrobe. There was no bioluminescence in this spot, and my body blocked the light from the rest of the tunnel, so it was all but impossible to make out the shape in front of me. Cautious, lest I injure myself again, I put my hands out.

As soon as my fingers came into contact with the heavy wooden door, I knew where I was. I found the strange brassy handle and pushed it open.

It was the first time I'd seen the tearoom so empty. The only people inside were myself and the waitress, and the windows weren't letting in any light. The fire and a series of colourful ceiling lights made the place feel warm and faintly yellowish. The waitress looked up from her closing duties and smiled at me.

"Kyle," she said, "don't mind me. Come on in—could you close the door?"

I did. "I, um… I just walked through a tree."

What else could I say? All the intelligence had completely gone out of me.

"Oh, is that where you did the summoning?" she asked. I got the impression she enjoyed watching me wipe my hands on my jeans to get rid of the dirt. "Haven't heard that one in some time. It's different for everyone, I suppose."

So, it could have been literally any kind of doorway. I asked where else the tearoom had turned up for people.

"Oh, all sorts of places. Wardrobes and garden sheds are popular. Occasionally someone comes in through a fitting room, and there's a cave in the Malvern Hills that's surprisingly popular. Actually, the view's quite lovely from there." She paused, then said, "I like it when people bring their pets. I miss having a dog."

I nodded sympathetically. "I miss my dog too. Uh—when you say 'us', is that, like, the 'royal we', or…"

The waitress offered me a wry smile. "Asking the important questions," she said. "I wish there were others here. It's just been me and the tearoom for… oh, about twenty years now."

"Twenty—how old *are* you? You don't look much over—"

"Nineteen."

She looked at me then, intensely, like there was more she wanted to say but couldn't. It took a moment to figure out what she meant. "That doesn't—wait. Are you trapped here?"

"It's just what this place does," she said, flipping a chair over and stacking it on one of the tables. She frowned and picked at a piece of gum some absolute charmer had stuck to the underside of the chair. "There's not much I can tell you along that line."

"Jesus."

"I know… but I'll leave. Eventually. I just need to be lucky."

"I… I see," I said, even though I didn't totally understand. "Hey, so, this might be a weird question, but why dusk? Is it, like, some all-powerful time or something?"

A sideways glance came my way. "Something like that."

"Oh." The waitress was watching me expectantly, waiting for more questions, so I continued. "How does this place do, you know, that thing? Like—how does it, you know…"

"Jump around? It took me a while to figure that one out, but I know the building is fixed in place, so it must be the entrance that moves. Don't look so surprised—you're the one who arrived through a tree. Is it really so hard to believe?"

At length, I said, "Suppose not. Where *is* the tearoom, then, if it's fixed in place?"

"Elphame."

51

I didn't recognise the name, but I felt like I should, somehow. "Where's that? Scotland?"

"You could say that."

That strange tone with the deeper meaning was back in her voice. As if there were other things the waitress wanted to say, but couldn't.

The fire was close to going out, I realised, and something was beginning to feel wrong. Without the hazy feeling and the smell of cinnamon, my senses were coming back to me. Something was, I realised with a jolt, *very* wrong. Beneath the nostalgia the fire caused, there was dread. As if I was somewhere I shouldn't be. Somewhere dangerous. The waitress frowned as I grabbed at the knot forming in my stomach.

"How long do I have to stay here?" I asked. The waitress gave me a nod, simultaneously understanding and deathly serious. She retrieved something from her apron pocket and threw it into the hearth.

"Kyle," she said as the fire roared back to life, clambering into the chimney in search of an escape route, making the room unbearably hot, "now you're asking the right questions."

Whether or not I blacked out is still up for debate. I'd never lost time after visiting the 4th Time Lucky before, but things were different this time. I don't remember a single thing between the fire springing furiously back to life and me waking up in an ambulance. There was a thermal blanket around my shoulders and a cup of something hot in my hands.

Dan and Matt sat either side of me. When I asked what was going on, Dan hugged me and wouldn't let go for a very long time. Matt gave me a strange look but didn't say anything.

It was almost dawn. He'd been crying.

Rex Alistair

The fourth time, you must be very, very lucky.

L ife went on. It was generally assumed that stress and depression had gotten to me, probably related to For Change, and that I'd had a breakdown and run away. I let people believe whatever they wanted; it was easier that way. I felt restless and slept poorly for a while, but that soon stopped, and despite my friends' worries, things would soon go back to normal.

Only Ryan knew the truth, although I suspected Matt knew something, too. We never did talk about it, although I could see he'd wanted to bring it up more than once.

A month or so after the whole summoning incident, Dan and Matt sat me down in the living room for what looked to be a serious talk.

There were two options here. One: they were announcing their engagement and wanted to give me a list of things not to say during my best man speech. Two: I'd become so good at poker they were worried I was doing things I shouldn't on Friday nights and wanted to hold an intervention. Both were equally likely.

"Kyle," Matt said, carefully, "we were thinking about doing a holiday after graduation."

"Oh," I said. "Cool."

"Thing is," Dan added, "we want to bring you, but we don't want it to be awkward for you. We were thinking about inviting Rachel along so you don't have to third-wheel or anything."

Ah. Theory One hadn't been too far off the mark after all. It turned out they'd forgotten to tell anyone. That was fair, I said, but I hoped they knew there would be a *lot* of teasing coming their way. Then I invited Rachel and asked her to help me tease them.

The four of us graduated and set off to the Isle of Wight.

Dan booked this time, so he finally got his cottagecore summer romance fantasy. I'm sure he was very pleased with himself.

The best thing about Rachel coming on holiday with us was that she could drive, and she'd just gotten a new second-hand car. This meant we didn't have to faff about getting our bikes on and off the ferry; we just whacked them on top of the bike rack and wondered off in search of food. Then we piled back into Rachel's car and Matt got us slightly lost a couple of times on the way to the cottage.

"God," Rachel said, "how do you remember your own name?"

He was Thomas for a while after that.

Rex Alistair

We finally found the cottage and got settled. There were three bedrooms; one for me, one for Rachel, and one for Dan and Thomas. Once the kitchen was stocked and all the bags were unpacked, it was decided that nobody felt up to cooking so we should go to the local pub for dinner.

That was when it started.

The cute little fashion boutique next to the pub wasn't a cute little fashion boutique anymore. The sign over its windows read 4TH TIME LUCKY.

The worst part was that nobody else noticed. They didn't notice how it was popping up everywhere we went, usually just around the corner or next to wherever we were going. It seemed to slip the minds of the others the moment they saw it, unless—and the thought of this kept me up at night—unless I was the only one who could see it. Maybe I should have asked, but I was afraid of the answer. What if they didn't see it? What if they did and wanted to go in?

It was probably the most stressful holiday I'd ever been on. I was determined to keep my friends from needing, or wanting, to go into that tearoom. There was something extremely wrong about the place, I knew that now, and I didn't want my friends to risk it.

Seeing the tearoom follow me caused something primal in the back of my brain to shake like a leaf. It was like watching a tiger stalk a child at the zoo, only there was no protective glass, and I had no idea when it would catch up or escalate things or what would happen when it did. I discovered, through the fog of my fear, an appreciation for why Ryan had made me go in first during my second visit. Ultimately, neither of us had signed up for this. I developed a semi-permanent stomach ache and stayed up long into the night, unable to sleep.

"Kyle," Rachel said, only a few days into the holiday, "are you alright? You look like death warmed up."

"Yeah," I lied. "Just weird being by the sea again."

I told her I was born by the sea and moved away when I was nine. My mum had actually gone into labour on the beach, or so I was always told. I used to stay up late and watch the ocean all night, then wonder why I had no energy the next day. I believed horses lived in the sea, and I believed the mist coming off it in the morning was thrown up by them running through the shallows at dawn. If I could just stay up long enough, I might be able to see them.

In retrospect, this might have been the reason I didn't go into shock after crawling through a tree. Part of me had always wanted to believe in magic.

Rachel said she hoped I wasn't trying to look for horses again. I said I wasn't and just couldn't sleep, she accepted my answer, and it wasn't brought up again. I tried to make myself look less tired so the others wouldn't worry. If they worried too much, I might let the truth slip by mistake. Following that, either they'd think I was crazy, or they'd want to go to the tearoom. Neither option was particularly appealing.

The holiday ended with nothing more to report, except that Rachel and I had decided we were going to be Dan and Matt's maid of honour and best man (they weren't engaged). We agreed to meet up every once in a while, we cried, and we prepared to go our separate ways. Dan and Matt moved to Birmingham together, Rachel went home to live with her family for a while, and I went back to the museum I'd worked at the year before. I had been offered full-time hours. The pay wasn't great, but rent nearby was cheap and it made me feel very grown-up.

Things went on as normal for a while, I got good enough at poker to help supplement my income a little, and I became used to seeing the 4th Time Lucky on a pretty much daily basis. Nobody ever went in or out.

It didn't bother me as much as it used to, except for the time I was running late to the last poker night before Christmas. The tearoom had taken the place of the damn pub. I couldn't even hear the usual drunken laughter from inside. Now, I had two options here: try the door and hope for the best, or turn around and go home.

I turned around and went home, sulking. It bothered me to no end that I didn't know who—or what—to be angry with. The waitress couldn't control where the tearoom went; she was trapped by it, much more literally than I was. If it wasn't her then there was an outside force making that stupid place follow me around, and *that* meant there might not be a way to make it stop.

Trying anything without knowing the full situation would be about as effective as screaming *knock it off* at a hurricane.

Oh well. As long as it didn't continue getting in the way like that, I could deal. Well, I *would* deal. Plenty of people got used to much stranger, after all, right?

My phone began ringing when I was about halfway back to my flat. Ryan, who'd been promoted to running poker night and was an excellent dealer, was calling to check on me.

"We saw you walk away," he said. "Everything alright?"

"Oh—er—yeah," I lied. "Just tell everyone I saw a weird ex."

"Ah. I'll let them know. Was it You Know Who?" It was nice of Ryan not to mention it in a way that might draw suspicion. He knew I didn't have any exes because I don't experience romantic attraction, so the next option was the tearoom.

"Yeah, it was," I said. "Thanks. I appreciate it."

"All part of the service. Pity, though. Got you a Christmas present."

"Oh—you didn't have to—"

"Yeah, well, that's too bad, innit? Anyway I'll give it you next time. You have a good Christmas, alright?"

"Yeah… you too."

It was only a couple of weeks later, when I returned to the pub with a pair of spectacularly ugly socks I'd bought just for Ryan, that I discovered the 'Christmas present' he got me was metaphorical. Rather, when I got there, he presented me with a flyer as ugly as the socks I'd picked out for him.

"Regional poker tournament in Brum," he announced. "You should sign up. Might do you a bit of good to get away for a few days."

According to the flyer, the tournament was in mid-February, so I folded it into my pocket and resolved to have a good think about it later. Whether or not I was any good, I could visit Matt and Dan while I was there.

A few weeks later, I checked into a spacious hotel room with about the funkiest headboard light I've ever seen. I unpacked, changed, and met Matt and Dan for dinner. We went out for Chinese; not the fanciest restaurant, but a lot nicer than we could afford back in uni. They looked happy together, despite the months of complaints I'd had from both sides about the housework. It had taken them a while to get into a proper routine, but now they'd settled and were doing much better.

"Can't believe you didn't visit sooner," Dan said. "Even Rachel's been up a couple of times."

"Yeah, I do feel a twit for not visiting," I said. The truth was that I'd been overworking myself to keep up with my bills and take my mind off the tearoom. I had plenty of holiday time saved up, I had Tuesdays and Wednesdays off, but I stayed in and didn't like to take any of them. I was terrified to have a repeat of the Isle of Wight. The stomach ache alone would probably do me in.

"You should've stayed with us," Matt said. "We wouldn't mind."

"Maybe next time," I said. "I don't know when the tourney ends yet. Can't have you two sitting up all night waiting for me.

"That'd be alright."

"It could be three in the morning."

"Ah—yeah, that's fair." There was a pause, then Matt asked, "Do you wanna do a Eurovision party with us?"

I smiled. "I mean, obviously."

"It's a costume party," Dan said. "You have to dress as extra as possible."

This was a little unusual for me, but I'd manage. We had a good dinner, promised to meet up again before I left Birmingham, and went our separate ways for the night. When I got back to my hotel room, I realised I hadn't seen the 4ᵗʰ Time Lucky since I arrived. I allowed myself to relax a little.

The poker tournament was the next day. There were twelve of us, all feeling rather rowdy and drinking as we exchanged greetings. One guy absolutely *stank* but, after enough drinks, I didn't notice anymore. Many, many more drinks were had over the course of the night. The smelly guy didn't do well and had a drunken tantrum. A few of us swapped contact details and promised to meet back up in a month or so.

We broke things up in the wee small hours of the morning. I had a fair bit of extra cash in my wallet—

my second-place prize—and unfortunately I was feeling rather cocky and became somewhat geographically challenged.

Lost. I was lost. I was *very* lost. The more I wandered about, the more lost I became. I couldn't even remember the name of the hotel I'd been staying in.

Unless it wasn't there on Friday nights?

Nobody said I was a particularly smart drunk.

I found a post I could lean on for balance, and tried to pull up a map of the city on my phone. Unfortunately, I was seeing triple at that point, and I managed to lock myself out of the damn thing. I saw the sign, all lit up like the front of a chip shop, when I glanced around in frustration. 4ᵀᴴ TIME LUCKY.

The fourth time, you must be very, very lucky.

Well, I'd certainly been very lucky today, and if I sat inside a while, perhaps I could sober up enough to find my hotel. I walked in.

Today, I was not the only patron. The waitress sat at a corner table, next to a sobbing, dark-haired man. She spoke low and slow, and she rubbed his shoulder as she did. His drink had gone cold a long time ago. It didn't feel right to butt in, so I sat near the fire and tried not to look at them.

The smell from the fire did help my head quite a bit. When the room stopped spinning so much, I leaned back and closed my eyes. Whatever was in the fire, it got up my nose and into my brain and pushed out most of the alcohol fuzzies. The waitress went into the back to make another drink for the sobbing man, and she placed a glass of water in front of me on her way back.

"Thanks," I murmured. She nodded and went back to comforting the man.

I began to entertain myself with the ceiling lights. The light shades were made from stained glass: blues and yellows and browns and greens and reds. They formed sweet images that seemed to move in the flickering firelight. A blue bee flitted between purple flowers; a red dragonfly hovered above an orange pond; a green spider spun a pink web. If I tilted my head just so, I could make them dance.

As I waited, my thoughts became clearer, and things began to make sense about the tearoom. I'd had to summon it at dusk because it made the tearoom's time sync up with my own. After all, hadn't the waitress said its fixed location was Elphame? That meant it ran on its own time, separate to the rest of the world.

Did they close at dusk, I wondered, or had I been in that tunnel a really long time? I wished I'd checked my watch.

The man left after an hour or so. I heard the waitress sigh as she slumped forward, her head dropping into her hands. She looked exhausted.

I switched tables to sit next to her and asked, "You alright?"

"It's been a long day, that's all."

"Ah."

"That was Henry. He just lost his son... he's going to want to come back very soon. It's not always easy, being here."

"Henry from California," I said. The waitress looked up at me. Her eyes were wide, brows knitted together. "Hey, uh, let me buy you some cake."

"Oh, Kyle, you don't have to."

"It's fine, I came second in a poker tournament and you look like you need something to eat."

"If you insist... what would you like?"

I love black forest gateau, and it turned out the waitress did too. I helped her plate up two slices and make a cup of tea, and we sat back down.

"You haven't been in a while," the waitress commented.

"Well... being stalked by a building kind of freaked me out."

"I understand that," the waitress said with a forced, harsh laugh. "You have to visit four times or it won't stop. It's one of the rules."

For a moment, I felt alarmingly cold. "Then—Matt has to come here three more times?"

"Matt's already been here four times. He and Dan got together between his third and fourth visits. Even your friends, Kevin and Ryan, have been here four times."

I hated how much sense that made. Matt *knew* I'd been back when I summoned the tearoom; that was why he was so upset. He knew it was going to happen to me. I wanted to tell him off for never bringing it up, even though I'd never brought it up to him, either. I was still going to kick him in the leg when I saw him next.

The waitress picked delicately at her food. She wasn't hesitant; probably just a slow eater. I was done long before she dropped her fork and said, "I don't mean to seem rude, but would you mind if I closed for the night?"

I understand wanting to be alone after a rough shift, so I said, "Oh, sorry—go ahead. I'll just be a minute."

We got up at the same time. I threw a couple of tenners on the counter, and the waitress produced a set of keys from her apron pocket. It would be a shame not to see her again. Something told me, as I opened the door, that she felt the same.

The waitress shot around me and slammed the door shut before I could step outside, but I'd already seen it. I hadn't opened the door to an early morning on the streets of Birmingham, but to a strange, wild landscape I'd never seen before. The sky out there had been purple, a permanent sort of dusk, and we seemed to be nestled at the base of a mountain. In the distance, I saw a deep, thick forest all around us. Those bluish lights from the tree root tunnel danced in the air. There were buildings dotted about far away: small cottages and cabins, some of which had lights flickering in their windows. Everything was tinged with purple, even the grass and the path leading away from the tearoom. The air was cool and smelled of wild garlic.

Rex Alistair

A dark feeling emanated from the purple world. It was the same feeling of intrusive danger... the one the fireplace was covering up. I turned to the waitress for an explanation. She looked like she was about to cry.

"Oh God, Kyle, I'm so sorry."

There is no fifth time.

I blinked stupidly and tried to say something. No words came out except:

"I didn't…"

The waitress shook her head. "I wanted you to be lucky, I really did."

Her fingers played with the knot on the back of her apron. She wanted to take it off, but she wasn't sure if she should. I dropped into a chair, something hot and dense settling in my gut. Another stomach ache was coming on. "But I… the poker," I argued feebly. It felt like I wasn't the one talking. "I was second place."

"I know." The waitress took a seat next to me. Her lips were pressed together, hard. "Would you mind if I stayed a while? I don't know what's waiting for me out there."

Her name was Martine Abbé. She was French. In fact, we were both speaking French right now. She didn't know where or when she'd end up when she left, and neither did I. "Sure," I said, weakly. My name was gone—I couldn't remember it.

"I've left a letter upstairs," Martine said. "There's a bedroom, and a bathroom, and a small study with books and a computer. I think you'll like it."

"Like it? I'm trapped here!"

"Not always. You can go out on Halloween, and there's a small garden behind the kitchen. You don't even have to restock things."

"That doesn't help, Martine."

She paused. She wanted to yell at me, but it felt so good to have her name back that she wanted to thank me for saying it. Instead, she went with, "It doesn't always last twenty-odd years. You might only be here a few months."

"There's no way to tell," I pointed out.

Silence. She agreed with me. I needed to be luckier than the next person. Would anybody even know I was gone? I had no partner to search for me. My only friends who knew about the tearoom couldn't come back, and the rules had made it so that they couldn't tell anyone.

"So I just have to wait?"

"Well... yes. Unfortunately."

"Great. That's just great."

"I've been through exactly this," Martine said. "It's not so bad, once you get used to it. You can't get sick, and you meet some really interesting people."

"It's not exactly my dream career."

"Then read history books. I'm trying, you know. I spent the last twenty years wishing the waitress before me had done this instead of running off the second I opened that door."

"I know."

Both feeling rather snippy and sorry for ourselves, we sat in silence for a while and finished off another pot of tea. Finally, Martine set her cup down and said, "I think I'm ready to leave."

"Right." I didn't want her to go. Not yet. I didn't want to be on my own.

"You'll be fine." The apron came up. "Everything's in the letter upstairs."

"Okay. Thanks."

Martine pressed her keys into my hand and said, "Do you know what happens when we leave the tearoom?"

I found that I didn't. Would she find herself in her own time or in mine? Would she still be nineteen, or would she age appropriately? I couldn't even say whether or not she'd remember the tearoom after she left. Ours was a very different circumstance to the one Ryan had been in.

She gave me a weak half-smile. "Then maybe you should look forward to finding out."

"Maybe," I said. All I could feel, then, was a reluctant sort of acceptance. Maybe I'd lock up, go upstairs, and have a little cry.

Rex Alistair

Martine Abbé did not say goodbye to me, nor I to her. She only looked back once, as she opened the door. Outside was noise; a crowded train station bustling with people, one of whom had just stepped out of a storage cupboard connected to the entrance of a very strange tearoom. Her last words to me, as she stepped into the frigid morning air and found her pockets weighted down with the tips she'd accrued over the years, were, "By the way—don't go into Elphame," and then she disappeared into the crowd.

Inside, I stood alone.

ABOUT REX ALISTAIR

Rex is a passionate, nonbinary author based in the West Midlands. A writer since childhood, Rex attended the University of Leicester and earned a bachelor's degree in English Literature with a minor Creative Writing.

In their free time and between writing projects, Rex enjoys reading, drawing, and spending time with their dog.

You can follow them on Instagram at @rexalistair

Printed in Great Britain
by Amazon

15786246R00041